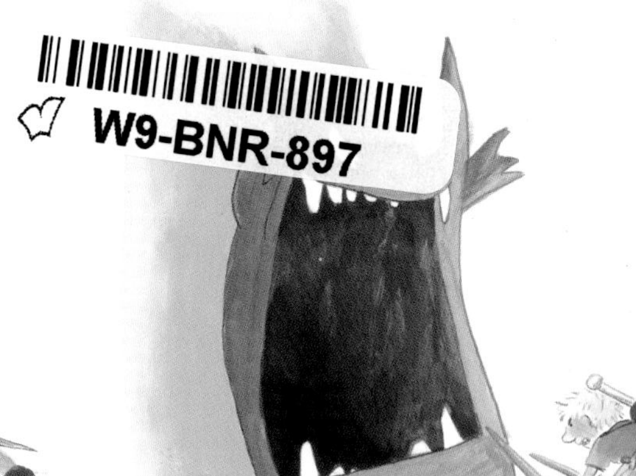

W9-BNR-897

Text copyright © 2004 by Cornelia Funke
Illustrations copyright © 2004 by Kerstin Meyer
English translation copyright © 2006 by Oliver Latsch

First published in Germany by Verlag Friedrich Oetinger, Hamburg © 2004

This edition first published in the United Kingdom in 2006 by
The Chicken House, 2 Palmer Street, Frome, Somerset BA11 1DS.
www.doublecluck.com

All rights reserved. Published by Scholastic Inc., *Publishers since 1920*, by arrangement
with The Chicken House. SCHOLASTIC and associated logos are trademarks and/or registered
trademarks of Scholastic Inc. THE CHICKEN HOUSE is a trademark of The Chicken House.

No part of this publication may be reproduced, stored in a retrieval system,
or transmitted in any form or by any means, electronic, mechanical, photocopying,
recording, or otherwise, without prior written permission of the publisher.
For information regarding permission, write to Scholastic Inc., Attention:
Permissions Department, 557 Broadway, New York, NY 10012.

Book design by Leyah Jensen and Ian Butterworth

Library of Congress Cataloging-in-Publication Data available
Reinforced Binding for Library Use

ISBN 0-439-82862-7
10 9 8 7 6 5 4 3 2 1 06 07 08 09 10

Printed in China
First American edition, May 2006

by Cornelia Funke

Illustrated by Kerstin Meyer

Translated by Oliver Latsch

WILDERNESS BRANCH LIBRARY
6421 FLAT RUN ROAD
LOCUST GROVE, VA 22508

The Chicken House

SCHOLASTIC INC./NEW YORK

Some mornings when Ben wakes up
he is a **WILD WOLF**.

Or a knight.

Or a **MONSTER** covered in **SCARS**.
He paints them on his face with Anna's makeup.
He always creeps very quietly into her room.
But sometimes Anna catches him.

Then she gives him a good tickling.
Anna is Ben's big sister.

Big sisters,
unfortunately, know
exactly where
little brothers are
ticklish.

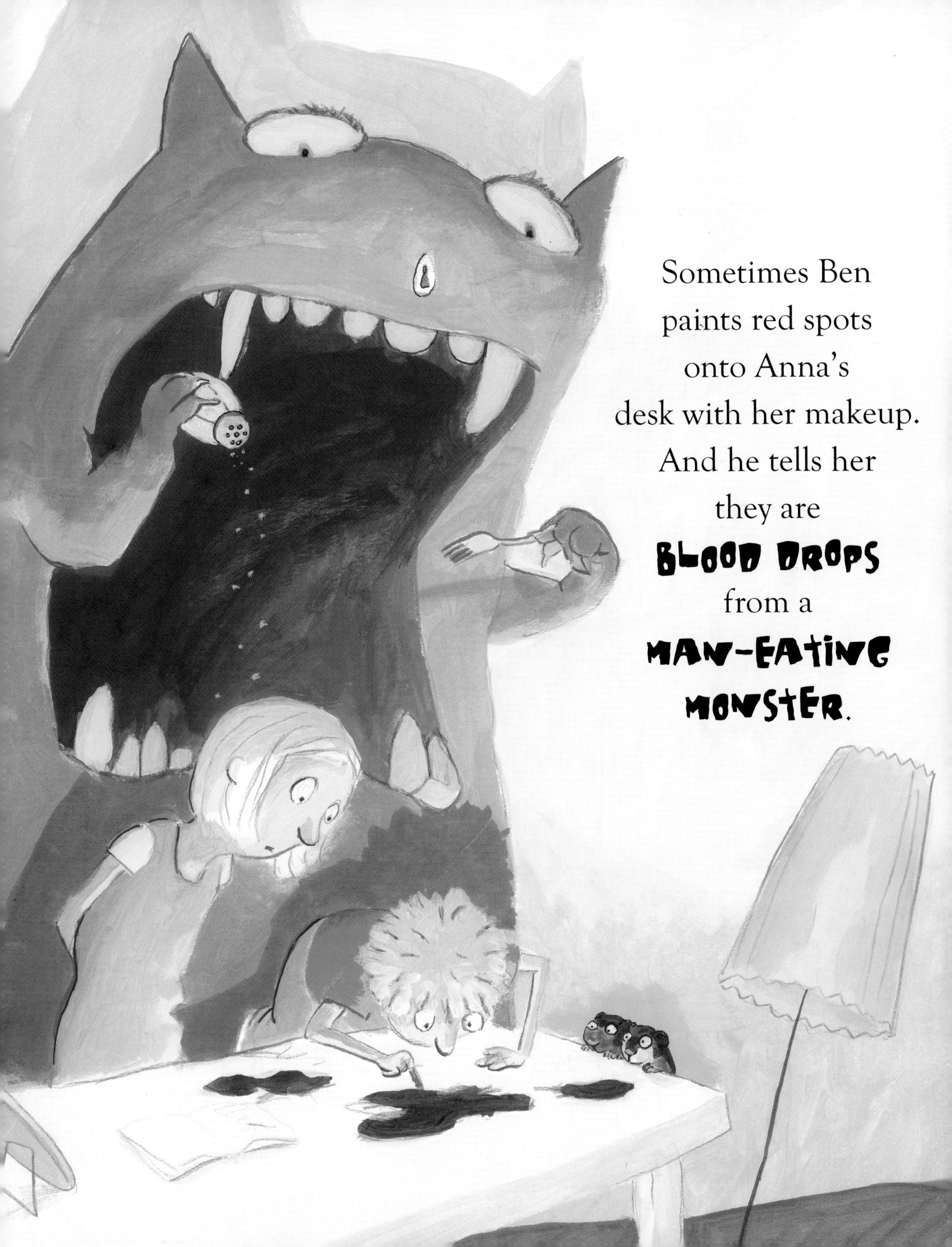

Sometimes Ben
paints red spots
onto Anna's
desk with her makeup.
And he tells her
they are
BLOOD DROPS
from a
**MAN-EATING
MONSTER.**

And that he'll protect her.
After all, he's lionhearted and elephant-strong.

Then Anna has to hide in the wardrobe.

Without giggling.

Because giggling makes monster-hunters terribly angry.

Anna is only allowed to make monster noises.

She's really good at it.

She GRUNTS and SNORTS and GROWLS.

And Ben, lionhearted and
elephant-strong,

fetches his
three plastic swords,
pumpkin-sized water pistol,
and rubber knife,

and fights until his face
turns bright red

and the

MAN-EATING MONSTER

is as quiet as a mouse.
Then Anna can come out
of the wardrobe again.

But Ben
can't stop to
wipe the
red spots off
Anna's desk.

Because
three
MOLDY
GREEN
GHOSTS
are still
HOWLING
in the
bathroom.

And Ben has to tear them to shreds
and flush them down the toilet—right now.

There's also the

SLIME-BURPING MONSTER

who loves to lick out

the pots in the kitchen.

Fearlessly Ben throws him off the balcony.

Then, using a jump rope, Ben ties up the **BURGLAR** who sneaks into the house once a week.

All this fighting is exhausting! So exhausting that once Ben even knocked one of Anna's horse posters off the wall.

But Ben does protect Anna from all the **FOXES** and **WOLVES** in the garden so Anna can pick dandelion leaves in peace for the guinea pigs.

Ben can't help Anna pick the leaves, though.
He has to keep an eye on the **BEARS** lurking
behind the bushes. They are just waiting
for the chance to **GOBBLE UP** such a tasty big sister.

Yes, Ben really has to fight quite a lot.
All day long, in fact.
His muscles have already grown big from it all.

But in the evening,
when Night
presses her soot-black face
against the window
and the heating creaks
like the sound of a thousand biting beetles,
Ben crawls into Anna's bed.
Then she protects him—
from Night's soot-black face
and the biting beetles.

And it is *sooo* wonderful
to have a big, strong sister.

These picture book favorites also available!

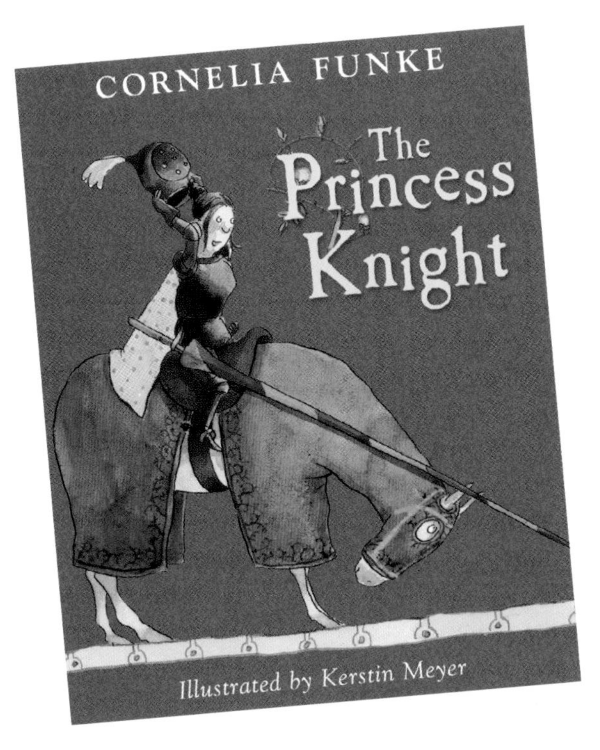

A fairy tale for tomboys!

★"Funke handles the picture book format just as deftly as her novels, with sure-footed pacing and a well-placed thrust through the cardboard princess stereotype."
—*Publishers Weekly*, starred review

★"So well done that it's likely to win over children who normally prefer their princesses without the revisionist twist....a jaunty parable with an endearing, indomitable character."
—*Booklist*, starred review and Editor's Choice

BOOK SENSE BOOK OF THE YEAR NOMINEE

CHILD MAGAZINE BEST BOOK OF THE YEAR

NEW YORK PUBLIC LIBRARY 100 BEST BOOKS FOR READING AND SHARING

The Princess Knight • 0-439-53630-8 • $15.95 US/$22.99 CAN

A glorious high-seas adventure that celebrates girlhood!

"Come aboard for a rowdy, satisfying seafaring adventure!"
—*The Horn Book Magazine*

"Funke and Meyer deliver a booster shot of girl power."
—*Booklist*

"Funke and Meyer convey the pirates' surly toughness while hinting at a fierce mother-daughter bond....{Molly's} like a Little Red Riding Hood of the high seas..."
—*Publishers Weekly*

SPRING 2005 PARENTS' CHOICE AWARD WINNER: PICTURE BOOKS

BOOKS FOR KEEPS MAGAZINE EDITOR'S CHOICE

Pirate Girl • 0-439-71672-1 • $15.95 US/$21.99 CAN

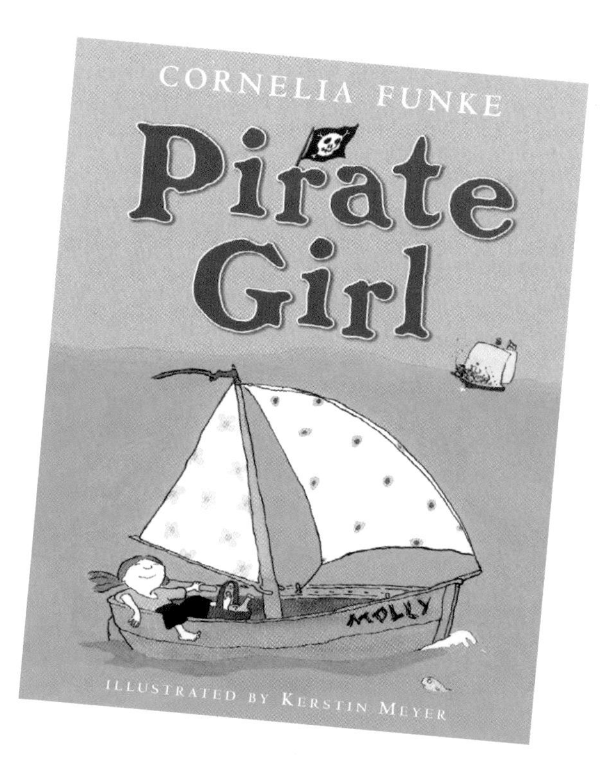

P Funke, Cornelia
FUN Caroline.
The wildest brother

MAY 07

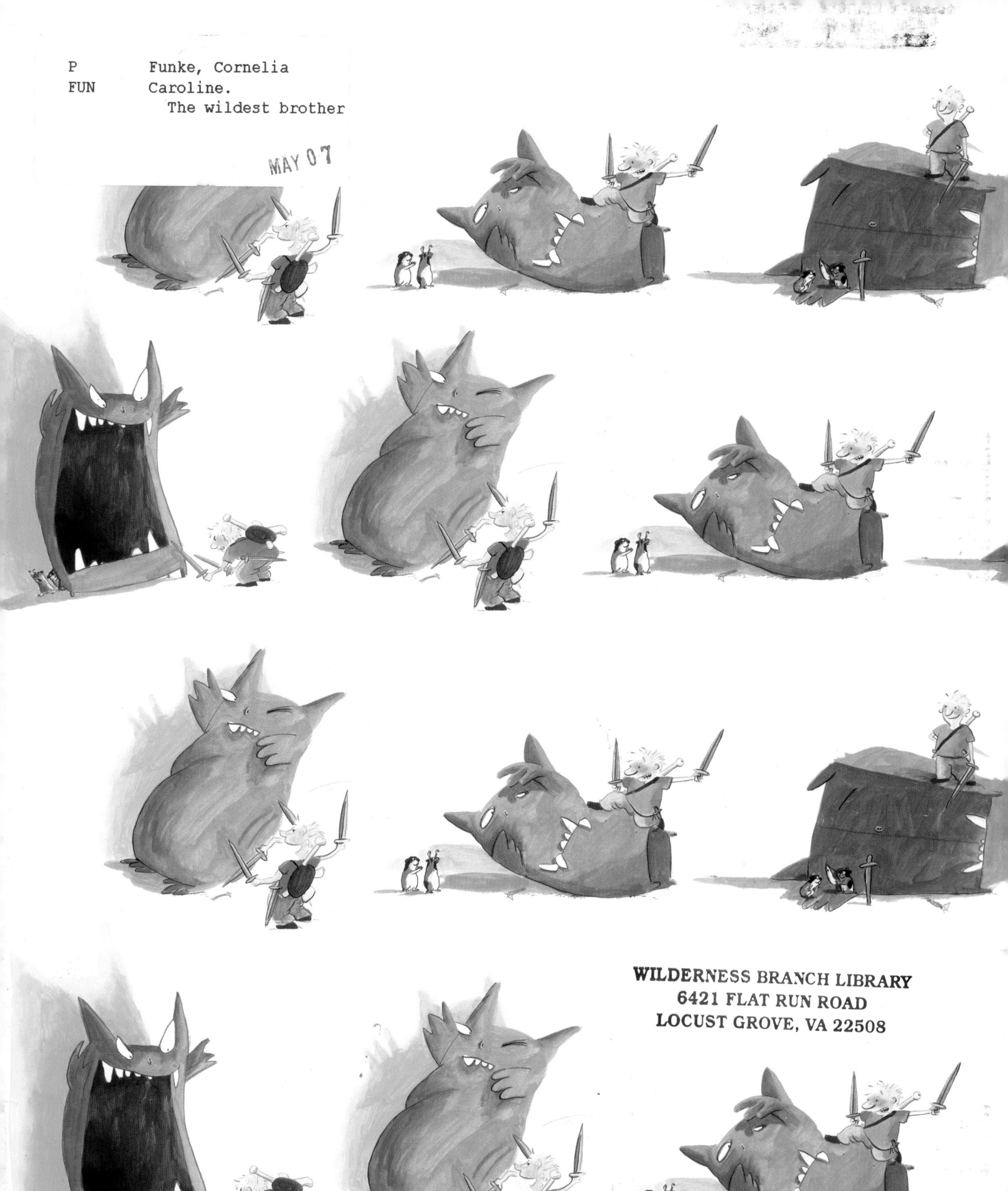

WILDERNESS BRANCH LIBRARY
6421 FLAT RUN ROAD
LOCUST GROVE, VA 22508